Tom
The Owl

Patsy Stanley

Copyright © 2020 to Patsy Stanley, author and illustrator of this book. All cover and interior art copyrighted to the author. Use of any part of this book without permission from the author or her representatives or agents is prohibited by law. All Rights reserved. No part of this book may be reproduced, transferred, modified, or used in part in any way and in any form without the express written consent of the author, Patsy Stanley, her agents or representatives. This book is a work of fiction.

ISBN 978-1-7356266-3-5

Tom the Owl and His Hollow Tree Home

Tom is a small, fluffy owl with big, curious eyes that always seem to sparkle with excitement. Tom lived in a magical **hollow tree** deep in the Whispering Woods. His home wasn't just any tree—it was the oldest tree in the forest, with roots that go on for miles and branches that tickle the stars.

Inside Tom's tree were cozy nooks and crannies filled with treasures he'd collected on his nighttime flights: shiny acorns, bits of feathers, and even a mysterious golden key. The hollow was warm and welcoming, glowing softly at night.

Tom's tree wasn't just his home; it's was also a library! Scrolls and books were tucked into the hollows of the bark. Animals from all over the woods come to borrow books and listen to Tom's stories. Tom had a special talent: he could read the stars, and they tell him tales of adventures, heroes, and magical lands.

One night, a storm blew through the Whispering Woods, and a loud crash woke Tom from his sleep. He discovered that the wind had brought a strange, glowing feather to his tree.

The Feather in the Wind

Tom blinked his bright eyes, still hazy from a dream of far-off starry skies. Outside, the Whispering Woods glimmered with raindrops caught in the moonlight. The storm had passed, leaving the air crisp and filled with the earthy scent of damp moss.

Something unusual caught his attention. Just below his hollow tree, nestled on a patch of glistening moss, is a feather unlike any he's ever seen.

The feather shimmered faintly, as though it held the glow of a thousand fireflies. It was long and golden, with edges that seem to ripple like sunlight dancing on water. Tom hopped down from his tree to take a closer look. As he approached, the feather seems to pulse with a gentle warmth, as if it carried the memory of sunlight within it.

Tom stretched out a wing and carefully nudged the feather with the tip. To his surprise, it felt alive—soft but sturdy, and faintly humming with energy.

A spark of curiosity lit in his chest. "Where could this feather have come from?" he wondered aloud.

Before Tom could pick it up in his beak, the feather flickered brighter and a faint trail of golden light appeared, pointing deeper into the Whispering Woods. Tom tilted his head, his curiosity growing stronger. He knew this feather was no ordinary find.

Clutching the feather gently in his talons, Tom spread his wings and lifted into the air, hoping to uncover the mystery of the glowing feather. The Whispering Woods stretch out below him.

The golden trail of light from the feather led him past familiar places—the bubbling creek where he liked to catch frogs, the old willow that always swayed in the wind. But as the light guided him deeper into the forest, Tom realized he was entering a part of the Whispering Woods he had never explored before. The trees here were taller, their twisted branches forming arches overhead, and the air seemed to hum with quiet magic.

Suddenly, the trail of light stopped in front of a towering oak tree with a hollow at its base. The feather in Tom's talons began to glow even brighter, illuminating the hollow. Inside, he saw a small nest woven with silver threads. Nestled in the center was an egg that shimmered with the same golden light as the feather.

Tom's heart fluttered with wonder. "This must be where the feather belongs," he whispered, dropping the feather carefully beside the egg. But as he pulled back, the feather flared with a brilliant light, and a voice—soft and warm—filled the air.

"Thank you, little owl," it said. "You have helped me find my way back."

Tom blinked, startled. Before his eyes, the feather rose into the air and gently wrapped itself around the egg, as if shielding it. Then the voice spoke again, softer this time. "The phoenix thanks you. One day, your kindness will be repaid."

Tom watched in awe as the glow faded, leaving the egg and feather nestled safely together. He felt a deep sense of peace as he flew back to his hollow tree, knowing he had been part of something extraordinary.

That night, as Tom drifted off to sleep, the Whispering Woods seemed to whisper their thanks. And somewhere deep in the forest, the phoenix egg began to warm, preparing for the day it would hatch and take to the skies.

Tom the Owl and the Lost Star

One chilly evening, as frost dusted the edges of the Whispering Woods, Tom the Owl perched on his favorite branch, gazing at the stars. The sky was unusually clear, and the stars twinkled like diamonds scattered across a velvet blanket. Tom loved stargazing; he often imagined the stars telling stories of faraway places and great adventures.

But tonight, something was different. As Tom tilted his head, he noticed a faint, flickering light moving erratically across the sky. It wasn't like the steady shimmer of the other stars—it wobbled and dipped, as if it were lost.

"What's that?" Tom muttered, narrowing his eyes. The flickering light grew brighter for a moment before suddenly plunging down toward the forest. A soft, distant thud echoed through the trees.

Tom's feathers fluffed with curiosity. "A fallen star?" he whispered. He had heard tales of stars falling to Earth, but he never imagined he'd see one himself. Without hesitation, he spread his wings and glided toward the direction of the light.

The forest was darker and quieter than usual as Tom flew, the only sounds coming from the soft rustling of the trees. He saw a faint glow through the branches. He swooped lower, landing on the forest floor near a small clearing.

There, nestled in a bed of moss, was a tiny star. It was no bigger than an acorn, its light pulsing faintly as if it were tired. The star shivered and let out a soft, chiming sound, like a bell far off in the distance. Tom approached cautiously. "Hello? Are you all right?"

The star flickered weakly, its light dimming. "I... I fell," it said, its voice as soft as the wind. "I've lost my place in the sky, and now I don't know how to get back."

"Don't worry," Tom said. "I'll help you."

"But how?" the star asked, trembling. "The sky is so far away."

Tom thought for a moment, his sharp eyes scanning the forest. "First, we need to make sure you're strong enough to shine brightly again. Stars need light, and there's plenty of moonlight tonight. Let's find a place where you can soak it up."

Tom carefully picked up the star in his talons, its warmth tingling against his feathers. He flew to the highest hill in the forest, where the moonlight bathed the land in silver. Placing the star on a smooth, flat rock, he watched as it slowly absorbed the light, its glow growing steadier.

"Feeling better?" Tom asked.

"A little," the star admitted, its voice stronger now. "But I still don't know how to get back to the sky."

Tom tapped his beak thoughtfully. "I think I know someone who can help."

He flew the star to the tallest tree in the forest, where the wise old Night Wind often passed by. The Night Wind was said to carry whispers from the heavens and knew the secrets of the skies. As Tom reached the treetop, the Night Wind stirred, rustling the leaves with its arrival.

"Tom the Owl," the Night Wind said in a deep, swirling voice. "What brings you here?"

"This little star has fallen and lost its way," Tom explained. "Can you help it return to the sky?"

The Night Wind swirled around the tiny star, inspecting it. "Ah, a brave little one," it said. "I can carry it back, but it will need one final burst of light to guide its way. Tom, will you lend your feathers to light its path?"

Tom nodded. The Night Wind whispered a spell, and Tom's feathers shimmered with a silvery glow. The star's light flared brightly, reflecting the gift of moonlight and Tom's glowing feathers.

"Hold on tight," the Night Wind said to the star. With a gentle gust, it swept the star into the air, carrying it higher and higher until it disappeared into the night sky.

Tom watched as the star returned to its place among the constellations, shining brighter than ever. A soft voice floated down from the heavens. "Thank you, Tom. I will remember your kindness."

Tom nodded and blinked. He flew back to his hollow tree, feeling a quiet satisfaction. Somewhere in the sky, a star now shone brightly because of him, and he knew the Whispering Forest would have another story to tell for generations to come.

Tom the Owl and the Enchanted Acorn

It was a crisp autumn night in the Whispering Woods, and Tom the Owl was on one of his nightly flights, searching for treasures to add to his hollow tree collection. His sharp eyes scanned the forest floor, lit faintly by the glow of the crescent moon. The air was alive with the rustling of dry leaves and the soft calls of nocturnal creatures.

As Tom swooped low over a grove of ancient oaks, something unusual caught his attention. Among the scattered acorns on the ground, one shimmered faintly with a golden light. Tom tilted his head, curious, and landed softly beside it.

The acorn wasn't like the others. Its smooth shell seemed to glow faintly, and delicate runes were etched into its surface, patterns that glimmered like tiny stars. When Tom leaned in to inspect it more closely, a soft voice whispered from the air around him.

"Help me," the voice said, faint and trembling. Tom hopped back, startled, his feathers fluffing with alarm. "Who's there?" he called out.

The glowing acorn trembled slightly, its light pulsing in time with the whispered voice. "It's me," the voice said. "I'm under a spell. Please, take me to the Forest Heart."

Tom blinked, unsure what to make of this strange request. He had heard tales of the Forest Heart, the oldest and most magical tree in the woods, said to be hidden in a secret grove. But no one he knew had ever seen it. "How do I find it?" Tom asked. The acorn's glow brightened, and the runes on its surface shifted and swirled into a new pattern, forming the outline of a tree. "Follow the path of the silver leaves," the voice said. "But beware—this journey is not without danger."

Tom felt a flicker of doubt, but his natural curiosity and sense of adventure won out. Gently, he scooped up the acorn in his talons and took to the air, his wings carrying him silently through the forest.

As he flew, a faint trail of silver leaves appeared below him, glinting in the moonlight. The trail twisted and turned, leading him deeper into the woods than he had ever ventured before.

The air grew cooler, and the trees seemed to whisper as he passed, their branches swaying in an unseen breeze. Suddenly, a shadow darted across the trail, and Tom froze mid-flight. Perched on a gnarled branch ahead was a large raven, its black eyes gleaming in the dark.

"What do you have there, little owl?" the raven croaked, its voice harsh and mocking. "Something shiny, I see. Why don't you give it to me?" Tom clutched the acorn tighter. "It's not yours," he said firmly. "I'm taking it to the Forest Heart."

The raven let out a sharp laugh. "The Forest Heart? Oh, how noble. But I think that treasure is wasted on you." With a powerful beat of its wings, the raven lunged toward Tom, its talons outstretched. Tom dodged just in time, weaving between the branches as the raven pursued him. The chase was fast and frantic, with Tom using his agility to stay one step ahead. "Hold on!" he whispered to the acorn, its glow flickering with urgency. Tom spotted a hollow in a nearby tree and darted inside, pressing himself against the bark as the raven swooped past, missing him by inches. The raven circled a few times, cawing in frustration, before giving up and flying away.

Tom waited until the forest was silent again before emerging from the hollow. "That was close," he said, his heart still racing. The acorn pulsed gently in his talons, as if in agreement.

The trail of silver leaves resumed, leading Tom to a grove surrounded by ancient oaks. At the center stood the Forest Heart, a towering tree with bark that shimmered like gold and branches that stretched high into the heavens.

Tom landed softly at its roots, where the ground glowed faintly with an otherworldly light. As he placed the acorn on the ground, the runes on its surface began to glow brighter, and the tree itself seemed to hum with life.

A soft, golden light enveloped the acorn, lifting it gently into the air. The voice returned, stronger now. "Thank you, brave owl. The spell is broken."

Before Tom's astonished eyes, the acorn transformed into a tiny, glowing sapling. Its leaves sparkled like diamonds, and its roots sank gently into the glowing earth at the base of the Forest Heart. The voice spoke again, this time with warmth and gratitude. "You have saved me, and for that, the Whispering Forest will always remember you."

The Forest Heart's branches swayed as if in agreement, while a single golden feather drifted down from above. Tom caught it in his beak, feeling its warmth and magic.

As he flew back to his hollow tree, Tom felt a deep sense of wonder. He had not only helped the enchanted acorn but also become a part of the Whispering Woods' ancient magic. And though he didn't yet know how, he was certain the golden feather would play a part in his next adventure.

Tom and the Shadow Stone

It was a very quiet night in the Whispering Forest. Too quiet, thought Tom the Owl as he perched on a high branch. Usually, the forest was full of sounds—rustling leaves, chirping crickets, or the soft hoots of other owls. But tonight, everything was still.

Tom tilted his head, his sharp ears picking up a faint hum. It sounded like a low, faraway song. Curious as ever, Tom spread his wings and glided silently toward the sound. The air felt heavier as he flew, and the trees below him looked older and twistier than he remembered.

Finally, Tom landed at the edge of a clearing. At its center stood a tall stone covered in moss and strange, glowing symbols. The hum was coming from the stone, and the ground around it seemed to shimmer faintly. Tom fluffed his feathers, unsure what to make of it.

"What is this place?" he wondered aloud.

Suddenly, a deep voice spoke, making Tom hop back in surprise. "This is the Grove of Shadows."

Tom turned to see a tall figure step out of the darkness. It was cloaked, with glowing eyes that looked like tiny red lanterns. "Who are you?" Tom asked, his feathers ruffling nervously.

"I am the Guardian of this grove," the figure said. "Few creatures come here, for this is the home of the Shadow Stone."

Tom blinked. "The Shadow Stone? What's that?"

The Guardian pointed to the glowing symbols on the tall stone. "Long ago, this stone was sealed away because its magic was too powerful. It could bring darkness to the whole forest if it were to break free."

Tom's heart skipped a beat. "Is it trying to escape?"

The Guardian nodded slowly. "The stone has grown restless. If it is not calmed, its shadows will spread."

Tom puffed out his chest. "What can I do to help?"

The Guardian looked at him thoughtfully. "The Shadow Stone can only be soothed by a song—a true song of peace and courage. But beware, little owl. The shadows will try to stop you."

Tom nodded. "I'll do it. The Whispering Forest is my home, and I won't let it fall into darkness."

Tom's Song

Tom hopped closer to the stone, perching on a low branch beside it. He thought of all the things he loved about the forest: the rustling leaves, the shining stars, and the gentle streams that bubbled through the trees. Taking a deep breath, he began to sing about them.

Tom's soft owl hoots rose into the night, telling a story of the Whispering Forest's beauty and balance. At first, the clearing seemed to grow brighter, but then the shadows around the stone began to stir.

Dark tendrils crept toward Tom, whispering in low, raspy voices. "Why bother, little owl? You're too small. You can't stop us."

Tom shivered, but he kept singing. His voice grew louder, stronger. "Even the smallest light can shine through the dark!" he sang, letting his words ring clear.

The shadows hissed and shrank back, but they didn't disappear. The humming of the stone grew louder, and the air around Tom swirled like a storm. The shadows lashed out, trying to silence him, but Tom thought of his forest friends and sang even louder.

He sang about the bright mornings, the cozy nights, and the harmony of all creatures working together. His song filled the clearing, pushing the shadows back further and further. At last, with one final, brave hoot, Tom's song reached the stone itself.

The shadows let out a long, wailing cry before dissolving into wisps of smoke. The humming stopped, and the stone's symbols dimmed to a soft, peaceful glow. The clearing fell quiet, but this time, it felt calm and safe.

The Keeper of the Grove

The Guardian stepped forward, its glowing eyes softer now. "You have done well, little owl," it said. "The Shadow Stone is quiet once more."

Tom ruffled his feathers, relieved but tired. "Will it stay that way?"

The Guardian nodded. "For now. But the stone will always need someone to watch over it. Someone brave and wise."

Tom tilted his head. "Me?"

The Guardian smiled. "You've proven yourself tonight, Tom. The Whispering Forest is lucky to have you."

Tom felt a warm sense of pride as he looked around the clearing. It wasn't scary anymore—it was peaceful and full of quiet magic. "I'll do it," he said. "I'll protect this place."

From that night on, Tom visited the Grove of Shadows often, keeping the Shadow Stone calm with his songs. He had become more than just Tom the Owl.

He was now **Tom, Keeper of the Grove**, a protector of the Whispering Forest and its hidden magic.

And though he was small, Tom knew his courage made a big difference.

Tom and the Forest Friends

After his brave song calmed the Shadow Stone, Tom began to realize he couldn't protect the forest all by himself. The Whispering Forest was a big place, full of mysteries and magic, and he knew he'd need the help of his friends to keep it safe.

One by one, the animals of the forest came to Tom, each eager to help in their own way.

Benny the Beaver: The Builder

Benny the Beaver was the first to join Tom's team. Benny was an expert at building and fixing things, and he loved to keep the forest streams flowing smoothly.

One day, Tom asked Benny to help strengthen the Grove of Shadows. "The Shadow Stone needs to stay safe," Tom explained. "Can you build a barrier to keep curious creatures from getting too close?"

Benny nodded eagerly. "Leave it to me!" Using sturdy logs and woven reeds, Benny built a beautiful wooden archway at the entrance to the grove. It looked like part of the forest itself, blending perfectly with the trees. Benny even added a little stream to flow around the stone, creating a soothing sound that helped keep the shadows quiet.

Lila the Fox: The Watcher

Lila the Fox had sharp eyes and a nose that could sniff out trouble from far away. She loved exploring the forest, darting between trees and slipping into places other animals couldn't reach.

Tom asked Lila to keep an eye on the forest's hidden corners. "If anything strange happens, let me know right away," he said.

Lila grinned. "You've got it, Tom. Nothing sneaks past me!" One night, Lila spotted a group of mischievous raccoons trying to get into the Grove of Shadows. They were drawn to the faint glow of the Shadow Stone, curious and unaware of its danger. Lila gently nudged them away, leading them to a patch of ripe berries to distract them. Thanks to her quick thinking, the grove remained undisturbed.

Mira the Moth: The Light Finder

Mira the Moth was small and delicate, with wings that shimmered like silver. She was quiet and shy, but she had a special gift—she could find light even in the darkest places.

Tom asked Mira to help him when the Shadow Stone's glow began to fade one cloudy night. "We need light to keep the shadows at bay," he said. "Can you guide me to it?"

Mira fluttered her wings nervously but nodded. "I'll try." She led Tom through the Whispering Forest, weaving through the trees until they found a patch of glowing stones. Tom carried a few back to the grove,

Tom and his friends became known as the **Guardians of the Grove**. Tom still visited the Shadow Stone often, singing songs of peace and courage. But now, he was never alone. With Benny, Lila, Mira, and Oscar by his side, Tom knew the forest would always have its protectors.

www.ingramcontent.com/pod-product-compliance
Lightning Source LLC
LaVergne TN
LVHW072022060526
838200LV00009B/232